When Baby Lost Bunny

For Margaret and John, my big brother and sister,
and our lovely mum! — J.J.

For Daniel Tomos Grace — A.R.

ORCHARD BOOKS
First published in Great Britain in 2011 by Orchard Books
This edition published in 2016 by The Watts Publishing Group

10 9 8 7 6 5 4 3 2

Text © Julia Jarman, 2011
Illustrations © Adrian Reynolds, 2011

ISBN 978 1 40834 675 4

Printed and bound in China

Orchard Books
An imprint of Hachette Children's Group
Part of The Watts Publishing Group Limited
Carmelite House, 50 Victoria Embankment, London EC4Y 0DZ
An Hachette UK Company

www.hachette.co.uk

www.hachettechildrens.co.uk

When Baby Lost Bunny

Julia Jarman   Adrian Reynolds

ORCHARD

We went for a walk,
Mummy,

Daddy

and me,

And Baby
in his buggy,

I gave Bunny to Baby,
Who smiled and said,

"Ug!"

Dad hoisted me high,
"Big Brother,
you're great!

What would we do
Without you to translate?"

"He was saying his bunny
Fell down by the gate."

Alone on the ground!

Baby's brown bunny

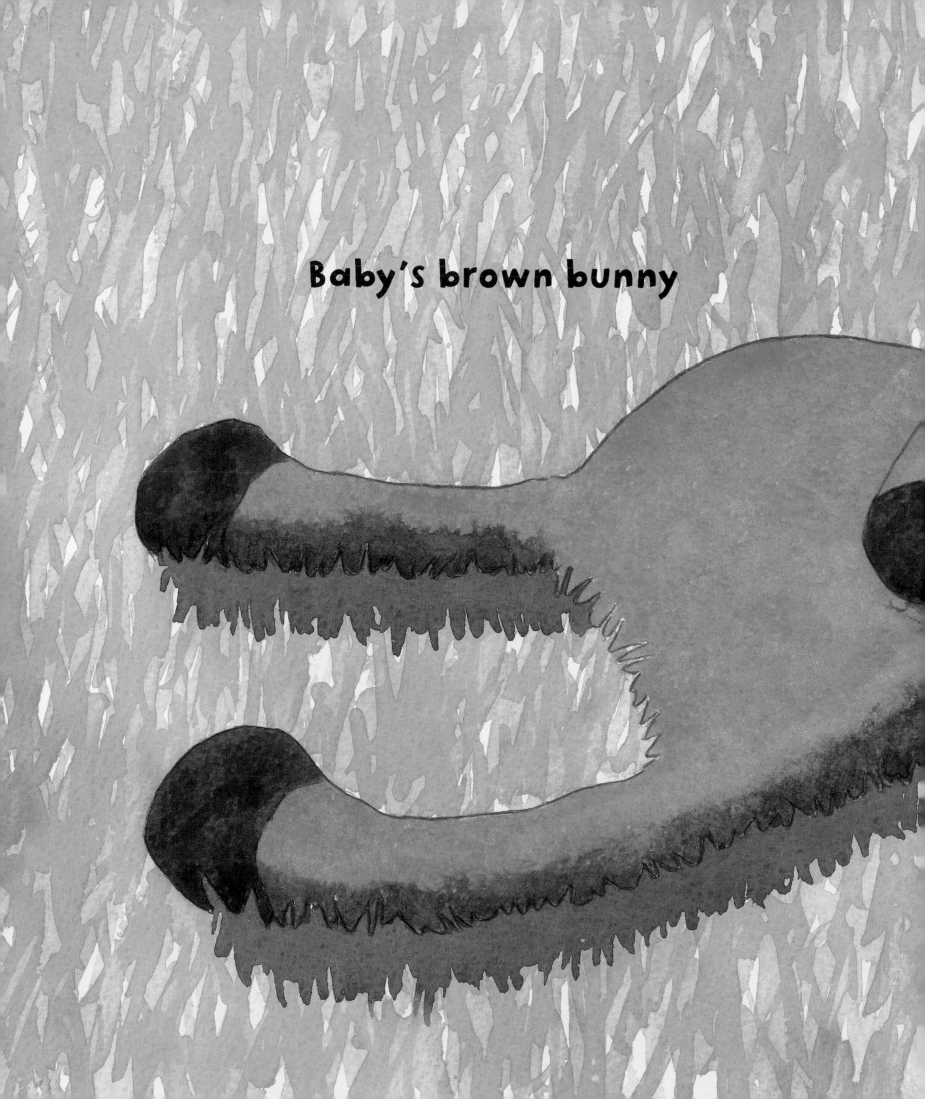

I looked and I looked
And at last I found . . .

Then, "Back in a minute!"
I started to run
As fast as I could
Back where we'd come.

"Waa waa!"

But I looked and listened
To what Baby said.

Dog looked at Daddy,
Mum shook her head,

Cat looked at the chicks,
The chicks looked at Hen,

Hen looked at Duck
Again and again.

Sheep looked at Cow,
Cow looked at Cat,

But none of them knew
What to make of all that.

But Sheep said to Cow,
"Baby didn't say 'Moo!'

Baby said,
'Baa!'
And to me,
not to you."

We all carried on walking,
But Baby started to cry,

We carried on walking,
Lots of us now,
And Baby bellowed, **"Ooo!"**

As we passed a cow.

"Miaow!"

said Black Cat,
And she followed us proudly.

Then Baby yelled,
"Myoo!"
Ever so loudly.

And Duck said,

"Quack! Quack!

I'm here, little fellow,
With Hen at the back!"

"Ack-ack!"

shouted Baby.

"Woof! Woof!"

said our dog.
"Yes, I'm here by your side!"

Then, "Oof-oof!"

cried Baby,
With his mouth open wide.

Then we did some more walking,
And Baby said,

And Mum said, "I'm here!

I'm pushing your buggy.
I'm here, little dear!"

Then Baby said, "Ma!"

And our dog, Mr D.

So I gave
my little
brother . . .